The Tennis Jock

By

ADRIAN M. HURTADO

Illustrated by Jayne Koontz

ISBN: 978-1-969865-21-3 (sc)
ISBN: 978-1-969865-22-0 (e)

Rev. date: 10/07/2025

Dedicated to athletes everywhere,
whether on the field, or in your mind

He shows up at the tennis courts
With racket in his hand
His clothing looks as if he just
Returned from Custer's stand

His left foot dons a high-top shoe
His right foot has no sock
He's ready to play anyone
He is the Tennis Jock

Singles
Only

He never plays with married folks
With couples never mingles
He's never been a married man
So only plays with singles

COURT 1

He's ready now to play someone
He thinks has lots of nerve
To stand there on the other side
And try to hit his serve

His first serve goes into the net
His second hits the fence
"No fair," he screams in outraged voice.
"I swung in self-defense."

He throws the ball up in the air
And misses with his swing
"I only missed the ball," he claims,
"Because I broke a string."

The other player's serving now
The score is Forty-Love
The Jock makes contact with the ball
And hits a bird above

"That point won't count,"
the Jock shouts out,
"That bird did interfere."
But the bird was 90 feet away
The tennis court's right here

He moves across the tennis court
Like a camel trying to waltz
He claims he scores a service ace
When his opponent double faults

The Jock is serving once again
He finally gets it in
He tries to hit the ball returned
But only hits the wind

He finally gets a volley going
Attempts a forehand drive
His racket hits him in the head
He's lucky he's alive

The ball comes back, he sets himself
For a backhand stroke
The way he swings, our Tennis Jock
Looks like a Tennis Joke

The tennis balls he brought for play
Are rather limp and flat
"That doesn't bother me," he says.
"I've got my game down pat."

So he plays all through the day
And never wins a game
Though, "Constant practice," he remarks,
"Is what has brought me fame."

The day is gone, he heads for home
This proud but weary Jock
And though he's sure he played so well
His games were just a crock.

www.ingramcontent.com/pod-product-compliance
Lightning Source LLC
Chambersburg PA
CBHW041144300726
48978CB00016B/1384